Unity Club

Karen Spafford-Fitz

Orca currents

ORCA BOOK PUBLISHERS

Library and Archives Canada Cataloguing in Publication

Spafford-Fitz, Karen, 1963–, author
Unity club / Karen Spafford-Fitz.
(Orca currents)

Issued in print and electronic formats.
ISBN 978-1-4598-1724-1 (SOFTCOVER).— ISBN 978-1-4598-1725-8 (PDF).—
ISBN 978-1-4598-1726-5 (EPUB)

I. Title. II. Series: Orca currents
PS8637.P33U55 2018   jc813'.6   c2017-907668-x
                    c2017-907669-8

First published in the United States, 2018
Library of Congress Control Number: 2018933727

Summary: In this high-interest novel for middle readers, trouble brews
when a group home for at-risk youth opens in Brett's community.
A free teacher guide for this title is available at orcabook.com.

*Orca Book Publishers is dedicated to preserving the environment and has
printed this book on Forest Stewardship Council® certified paper.*

Orca Book Publishers gratefully acknowledges the support
for its publishing programs provided by the following agencies:
the Government of Canada through the Canada Book Fund and the
Canada Council for the Arts, and the Province of British Columbia
through the BC Arts Council and the Book Publishing Tax Credit.

Edited by Tanya Trafford
Cover photography by iStock.com/Vincentguerault
Author photo by Photosmith Design

ORCA BOOK PUBLISHERS
orcabook.com

Printed and bound in Canada.

21 20 19 18 • 4 3 2 1

To my parents,
Rosemary and Jack Spafford,
who are deeply committed to their
family and to their community.

Chapter One

My phone vibrates on the kitchen counter. I glance at it as I bite into my bagel. As usual, my mom's texts are a combination of French and English.

Brettenie, you haven't texted me in a long time. *Tu me manques.*

She's the only person who actually

calls me "Brettenie." Everyone else calls me Brett.

"*Tu me manques*," I mutter. Yeah right, she misses me. Then how come she moved so far away?

Even though Papa left early this morning for a meeting, I look around to make sure nobody caught me talking to myself. But of course, I'm the only person here. Papa has thrown himself into his work ever since Maman left town. We've both kept extra busy. That way, we don't have much time to think about how she abandoned us.

I spot my math assignment on the counter. I'm sure I drew the stupid graphs wrong. My mom used to help me with my math. When she moved to Winnipeg, she told me to phone her whenever I needed help. As if.

I'm jamming the papers into my backpack when my phone buzzes again.

How's your new school? *Dis-moi!*

The chunk of bagel in my mouth suddenly feels even drier. Seriously? My school is hardly *new* anymore.

I've been going to Addison Junior High for four months now. But my mom's mind has been on other things—namely, her new boyfriend. She's right about one thing though. I haven't texted her for a long time. And I'm not about to start.

I toss my phone into my backpack. I throw the rest of my bagel into the garbage. Then I duck out the back door.

I used to take the city bus to Willow Heights Junior High. It was my mom's idea for me to go there. She was wowed by all the special programs. So for the sake of the school's travel-studies option (I throw up on airplanes), academic enrichment (dream on) and a dance program (not a chance) that I never took, I spent hours traveling to school on crowded city buses that made me want to barf.

After my mom left town, the first thing I did was switch schools. Now it only takes me ten minutes to walk to school—or six minutes if I run. I check the time on my phone—8:55. I'd better run.

As I turn the corner at the end of our street, I avoid looking at the big blue house with the For Sale sign out front. That's the house my mom bought three years ago, after she and my dad got a divorce. Their two houses were close enough together that I often visited both of them every day. It was totally working—until my mom met a guy on an online dating site.

The worst part is that this guy, Zoltan, lives in Winnipeg. That's a thirteen-hour drive from Edmonton. The next thing I knew, Maman took off to go live there with the new love of her life and his three kids. I shake my head. And she wonders why I don't return her texts?

"Brett! Hey, slow down!"

"Hey, Amira." I glance over my shoulder. "Come on. We're going to be late! Ms. Vickers said we had to hand in our math homework right at the beginning of class."

"We don't have to hurry," she says. "I heard Ms. Vickers left yesterday with a bad migraine. She called in a sub for today." Amira pauses to catch her breath. "The sub will be too busy sorting out attendance to notice if we're a bit late."

"Okay," I say. "If you're sure."

I let my angry thoughts about my mom fade from my mind. I slow down to a walk.

"So what about after school?" Amira asks. "Are you ready for the meeting?"

"Yeah, I made some notes last night."

"What will we be talking about today?"

"You'll have to wait and see," I tease.

Amira gives a pretend pout. The corners of my mouth tug upward into a smile as we walk the last few blocks to school.

When I transferred to Addison Junior High, the first thing I did was join the Unity Club. The Unity Club's goal is to make a positive difference in the world. We mostly volunteer in our community, but sometimes we do fundraising for different causes around the world.

As it turned out, joining the Unity Club was the best decision I've ever made. It has helped take my mind off my mom. It's also where I got to know the people who have become my new best friends. People like Amira. It isn't as dazzling as a dance academy. And it's maybe not as exciting as taking school trips to Spain. But I felt welcome right from the beginning. When Isabelle, the club president, moved away a couple of months ago, I was surprised to be nominated for the position. And then I got voted in as president. It's a lot of work, but we have some great projects on the go. I'm totally up for the challenge.

My phone vibrates in my backpack. I ignore it. Probably my mom again. Why can't she just leave me alone?

Chapter Two

After school, the Unity Club is meeting in the drama room. Some students are sprawled across the risers that the drama classes use for a stage. Other students are half lying and half propped against each other on the carpet beside the risers. A few of them are knitting.

"Hey, everyone. Let's get started," I say. "How about—"

Just then a tall boy with messy brown hair bursts through the door. Kaden has been a member of the club for two years now. When Isabelle moved away, Kaden was the only other person to run for president. I was brand-new to the school. I was as surprised as Kaden was when I got voted in. I suggested we share the job, but Kaden refused. I still remember what he said before he stormed out. *If everyone wants the new kid instead of me, then fine. Whatever.*

Today he's wearing his usual scowl.

"Okay, let's get started," I repeat. I avoid looking directly at Kaden. Otherwise it's too hard to keep my voice steady.

"First of all, our regular projects have been going great. I will be asking the leads on those to update us in a few minutes. But first I want to give a shout-out to our knitters. They've been working hard on our blanket project for the seniors' residence."

Other than Liam, Dionne and me, the other club members just recently learned how to knit. Eliza constantly drops stitches. Her knitted "squares" all have holes in them. And they are never even close to being square. It doesn't really matter though. With all the bright colors we're using, a few oddly shaped pieces will just add to the charm.

"Once we have enough squares, Mrs. Rashid says she'll help us stitch them together," I say. "Amira, can you give us an update? What else has the group been doing over at Fairview Court?"

"Last week," Amira says, "Brett, Justine and I took a cake over to celebrate all the seniors who have birthdays in January. We turned it into a tea party. Then we played Bingo together. Everyone seemed to have a good time.

Other than that," she continues, "we've all been focusing on finishing our squares."

"Don't remind me," Eliza sighs. "I just dropped another stitch!"

A groan goes up around the group.

"It's okay," I say. "I can fix it later. The seniors are going to love the blankets. We almost have enough now to give each of the new residents one for Valentine's Day. Every square helps."

"Ta-da!" Cohen holds up a navy-blue square he has just finished.

"I can think of a few squares that maybe won't help." Justine is trying to keep a tangle of green yarn from sliding off her needles.

I smile. "Are you guys still surprised that I can always tell who knit which square?"

"Let's test that out." Cohen reaches into the basket beside him. "Here's sample number one."

He holds up an orange square. It has way more stitches at the top than at the bottom.

"Easy," I say. "Suresh knit that one."

"Yep," Suresh says. "That one's mine."

Cohen takes out a red square. "Sample number two," he says.

The stitches on this one are pretty even. They aren't quite as straight as mine though. Maman taught me to knit when I was five. I've been doing more complicated stitches than this for years. This one has to be either Dionne's or Liam's. And since it's red—

"Dionne," I say.

"Wow," Dionne says. "We can't trip her up."

"Let's give her one more," Cohen says. "Just to be sure." He pulls out a forest-green square. "Sample number three."

"That's the easiest one yet!" I say with a grin. "It's mine!"

"How do you know I didn't make that one?" Eliza says. "It looks a lot like *this* one." She holds up her knitting. I can see the holes from where she's dropped some stitches.

I smile at her. "Hmm, just a lucky guess," I say. Everyone laughs. Except for Kaden, that is.

"Okay, next up is the Mini Gym Kids. Some of you have been taking the bus downtown to Lennox School." I turn to Liam. "Can you tell us how it's going?"

"Sure." Liam sits up straighter on the riser. "So far there are eighteen kids in grades two and three. Last week we played dodgeball and kickball."

"Wow," Amira says. "There were only five kids when we first started."

"I know," Liam says. "It's getting really popular. Some grade-one kids want to join in now too. That's at least another ten students."

"I'd like to include the grade ones if possible," I say.

"Me too," Liam says. "But we'll need at least three more volunteers."

"So far," I say, "our regulars at Mini Gym Kids are Liam, Eliza, Cohen and Amira. Can anyone else help out on Tuesdays after school?"

Nobody speaks up at first.

"Badminton club finishes in two weeks," Dionne says. "I can help after that."

"I can probably move my piano lessons to Wednesday," Justine says.

"Good," I say. "Anyone else?"

Kaden hasn't said anything since he arrived. Is he waiting for me to ask him?

I decide to go for it. "How about you, Kaden?" Was it just my imagination, or did he almost smile?

But then the usual dark cloud settles back over his face. "I can't do it," he says. "I think *you* might be on for it, Prez."

My face flushes. "I'll be super busy making the blankets for the seniors. Even with Mrs. Rashid's help, it's going to be a lot of work." I hesitate. "But sure. I guess I can do Mini Gym Kids too."

Kaden is at the back of the room. Still, I can see the smug look on his face. What a lousy attitude! Maybe it would be better if he just quit the club.

I feel guilty the moment that thought crosses my mind. The Unity Club is supposed to include everyone who wants to participate.

I take a deep breath. "Let's hear from the last group." I turn to the girl sitting nearest me. "Georgia, can you update us on our environmental projects?"

Georgia sets her knitting down. "We're trying to get the whole school to think and act more responsibly when it comes to our environment. We've posted facts and figures on the school's website. Tassie, Suresh and I also wrote some announcements. We're going to read them over the PA system once a week."

Tassie nods. "I think it's going well," she says. "We've also placed extra recycling bins around the school. Both the students and the teachers have been using them more."

"Our next focus," Suresh says, "will be on how to reduce the amount of water we use. We've also started planning Earth Day celebrations."

"Good work, you guys," I say as I glance over my notes. "I think that's it for today. Once again, it would be great if we could get a couple more volunteers to come to Mini Gym Kids on Tuesday afternoon. Otherwise, see you next week."

Kaden leaves without saying a word to anyone. The others drift out of the drama room, except for Amira. She waits for me while I stuff the new knit squares into a bag to give to Mrs. Rashid.

On our way home, I look around to make sure no one else can hear us. "You know," I say, "I don't know what to do about Kaden."

"Don't even worry about him." Amira shakes her head. "You offered him the chance to be club president too. He said no. And he shouldn't have put you on the spot about the Mini Gym Kids."

"I think that was wrong too," I say. "But still—"

I've been thinking so much about Kaden that I forget to look away when we get to the big blue house. Serious mistake. Because today the For Sale sign on the front lawn has a big red Sold sticker across it. I freeze.

"What is it?" Amira asks.

"Nothing really. It's just—I used to know the person who lived here. But I don't really know her anymore." I'm fighting to keep my voice steady.

I tug Amira past the house. I'm glad she doesn't know who used to live there. I can't bring myself to talk about it—not even with my best friend.

Chapter Three

On the days that I have Unity Club meetings after school, Papa usually gets home first. He is a French professor at the university. Because a new term just started, he has a lot of meetings. He's been getting home later than usual most nights. I can tell he is also trying to keep extra busy since my mom left town.

There's no sign of Papa when I get home, so I start making dinner. Neither of us is a very good cook. We mostly left it to Maman. She used to make the most awesome grilled cheese sandwiches and homemade pizzas. On special occasions, she would whip up fancier dishes. My favorite was *tourtière*. Just thinking about that delicious meat pie makes my mouth water. I wonder if she's made it for Zoltan and his three screaming brats.

Okay, maybe they're *not* screaming brats.

Still, I prefer to think of them that way. Better to stay angry. Then it doesn't hurt quite so much that my mom is spending her days with them instead of with me.

I measure out some rice and add it to a pot of water on the stove. Then I pull out the usual three ingredients from the fridge—chicken, onions and red peppers. As I chop everything up, my mind circles back to the Sold sticker on the sign in front of my mom's house. Maybe that's what one of her texts was about.

With the chicken and vegetables now sizzling in the frypan, I grab my phone. I scroll through all my unopened texts. Sure enough, there it is.

J'ai vendu la maison.

I sold the house. So she *did* try to tell me before the sign went up. Still, I don't feel any better.

I grab a jar of spicy Thai chili sauce from the cupboard. I dump it over the chicken and veggies. This is how my dad and I try to "vary our diet." I've heard we're supposed to do that. So we buy different sauces from the international aisle at the grocery store. Then we pour them over our chicken and vegetables.

I'm stirring everything together when Papa comes into the kitchen.

"*Bonjour, chérie*," he says. "You've made dinner already? *Parfait!*"

Papa sets down his laptop and briefcase. While he peels off his coat, he glances at me over the top of his little round glasses.

"Did you notice the sign in front of your mother's house?" Papa is trying to be gentle. But he must know that I couldn't have missed it.

"*Oui*," I say.

The silence hangs in the air between us. Papa is shuffling about the kitchen and rubbing his gray-brown beard. He always does this when he's upset. He's been doing it a lot lately.

"Are you okay about that?" His face is serious.

"I don't have much choice." I try to say it lightly. After all, the divorce wasn't my dad's idea. And, like me, he wasn't thrilled when my mom announced she was leaving town.

Papa sighs. "*Désolé*, Brett. This probably feels extra final now that someone has bought your mother's house."

I nod, still keeping my gaze directed at the stove. "Yes. But it's not like I thought she was ever coming back…"

My voice drifts off. I realize that's exactly what I hoped would happen. I shake my head. *Come on, Brett. It's not like you're six years old and don't know any better.*

When we sit down at the table, I mostly move the food around on my plate. As soon as Papa finishes eating, I set down my fork too.

"I'm going upstairs," I say. "I have a science assignment to finish."

Papa is rubbing his beard again. "Do you want to talk?" he asks.

"*Non.*" I shake my head.

Papa looks relieved. But he looks sad too. "Okay," he says with a sigh. "You go ahead. I'll clean up."

Upstairs, I flop onto the bed and pull out my phone. Even though I'm still not going to reply to Maman, I scroll through her texts again. I learn that Zoltan's kids are at their mother's place tonight. My mom and Zoltan are having a quiet dinner together. Definitely more information than I need. Also, she tells me they are planning to watch the hockey game on TV. Really? Since when did she become a hockey fan?

Maman also says that Zoltan is a good cook. That he made cabbage rolls last night. Who cares? Part of me wants to tell her that for months now, Papa and I have been eating the same four ingredients a dozen different ways. Maybe that would get her attention. Then I remember that I'm not giving her the satisfaction of replying to her texts.

I toss my phone aside and wipe away the tears streaming down my face. Clearly my mother has moved on with her new life. And no matter how many texts she sends me, her new life does not include me.

Chapter Four

In the days ahead, I look the other way whenever I pass my mom's house. Most mornings Amira has caught up to me by the time I get to that corner. Her chatter helps tide me over. But today she must be running late.

Maybe it's dumb, but I've actually been wondering if I will feel better if I sort of say goodbye to Maman's house.

I come to a complete stop in front of it. Then I take a few steps up the driveway. I take a hard look at the front bay window that catches the morning sun. At the porch that wraps around the front and side of the house, where we used to read. At the little blue spruce tree that we planted together in the front yard.

With four bedrooms, this house was way too big for just the two of us. But Maman always said it was perfect because it was close to Papa and me. Now some house across the country is perfect, apparently. Despite the wind and the swirling snow, heat is building inside me.

"Can I help you with something, miss?"

I spin around. The man standing behind me is zipping up his parka.

"No, that's okay," I say. "Um, are you the new owner?" I nod toward the house.

"No."

"Oh, sorry," I say. "I assumed that because the house just sold..."

"Actually, this house is being converted into a group home for teenagers," he says. "I'll be working here soon as a supervisor. I'm Mike, by the way."

"I'm Brett." I pause to think about what he said. "So this place will be for kids who don't live with their parents?"

"That's right." Mike hunches his shoulders against the cold. "We're starting renovations to create six bedrooms for the teenagers. The house is pretty big. We just have to add a few walls to make two extra bedrooms. It already has all the bathrooms and parking spots we need."

I know exactly the spaces he's talking about. I'm still angry that I don't get to live here with Maman anymore. But it does seem good that some other teenagers will get to live in the house.

Especially since they probably have worse problems than I do.

I'm about to move on when I hear a voice behind me.

"A group home for teenagers? You're kidding me, right?"

I turn and see Mr. Jamieson. He lives just down the street. He's scowling, and his arms are crossed.

"The community is *not* going to like that," he continues. "Definitely not on our street."

"Why not?" My voice sounds tiny and choked.

"Because I know exactly what's going to happen once a gang of teenagers moves in. Property damage. Noise. Partying all day and night. And the value of our homes will fall." He's counting these things off on his gloved hands as he speaks. "Trust me, this is *not* a good idea."

"Then where will those teenagers live?" I ask.

"I realize they need to live *somewhere*," Mr. Jamieson says. "But anywhere other than this neighborhood would suit me just fine." With that, he stomps off down the street.

I'm too angry to speak. Mike looks almost as shocked as I do.

I take a deep breath. "I'm really sorry about that," I say. "I think Mr. Jamieson is wrong. I think building a group home here is a good idea. And I think the rest of the neighborhood will agree."

"I hope so." Mike shakes his head. "Unfortunately, NIMBY is a common response."

"NIMBY?"

"Yes. NIMBY is short for *not in my backyard*. It's when people agree with the idea of something—like having a safe place for teenagers to live—but not if it's going to happen right in their neighborhood. Or anywhere near where they live. They're afraid they might be affected personally."

"Well, I think that attitude stinks." Something else occurs to me. "Just wondering…the teenagers who move in here—will they be coming to Addison Junior High?"

"Probably," Mike says.

Hmm. Maybe this is something the Unity Club can help with.

"Hey, Brett!"

I turn and see Amira hurrying toward us.

"I'd better let you get to school," Mike says.

"It was nice to meet you, Mike."

As Amira and I walk to school together, Mr. Jamieson's words keep running through my mind. I can't wait for the kids from the group home to start attending classes at Addison. And for Mr. Jamieson to realize that he is wrong.

As usual, the Unity Club members are sprawled on the floor and across the risers in front of me.

"Last week," I say, "Mrs. Rashid and I got all the squares stitched together in time for Valentine's Day. A group of us wanted to take the blankets over to Fairview Court. But they've had a flu outbreak."

"Oh no!" Suresh says. "I've heard the flu can be dangerous for elderly people."

"Yeah," Amira says. "Like for all the seniors who live there."

"Exactly," I say. "So they're not allowing any visitors at Fairview for the next couple of weeks. So I just dropped off the blankets at the front desk."

"It's awesome that we got the blankets done in time," Amira says. "Hurray for us!"

A cheer goes up around the room. I wait a moment before I move on to the next point.

"We have some new business to discuss." I try to keep my voice even as I remember Mr. Jamieson's words. "A house down the street from where I live is being converted into a group home for teenagers. Some renovations are already happening there. The teenagers will be moving in soon. Some of them will probably register here at Addison."

"That sounds great," Dionne says.

"I think so too," I say. "I talked to a man who's going to be working there. I also did a little online research. Kids who live in group homes often don't have parents who can care for them. Or sometimes the teenagers have problems that mean they can't live at home anymore."

"That must be so hard," Cohen says.

I nod. "These kids have already been through a lot. And now they have to switch to a new school. Since the Unity Club is all about compassion and community involvement, I think it's up to us to make them feel extra welcome here."

Everyone takes a moment to think about this. Amira is the first to speak up. "Maybe some of them would even like to join our club."

"That would be great," I say. "We can't push them. But if you get to know any of the students, you could invite them to join us."

"It's too bad we already gave away all the blankets," Dionne says.

"Yeah," Suresh says. "Some of these kids might not have many personal belongings when they get to the group home."

"Or many clothes," I say. "And since it's still cold out, maybe we could make them hand-knit scarves instead."

"That's a great idea," Amira says. "A personal gift that also helps keep them warm."

"Yeah," Liam says. "Scarves knit up pretty fast."

"Maybe for some of you," Eliza says.

I decide not to tell them what Mr. Jamieson said. I want to keep things positive.

Hopefully, Mr. Jamieson is the only person who won't want them living here.

Chapter Five

I was going to ask Mrs. Rashid if she would knit a scarf too. But then I learn that she has come down with the flu. She isn't allowed any visitors until she has fully recovered. So the Unity Club is on its own for this new scarf project. In the days that follow, I knit like crazy.

On my way to and from school, I've seen more and more people coming and going from the old blue house. New students could arrive at Addison any day.

"*Mon Dieu*," Papa says. "You're knitting hard." He dumps yellow curry sauce over tonight's chicken, onions and peppers.

I finish knitting the row I'm on. Then I take the rice off the stove and dish it out.

"Yeah, we're knitting scarves for the kids who are moving into Maman's old house," I say. "You know it's going to be a group home, right?"

Papa nods. "*Oui*. I've heard some talk around the neighborhood about it."

Oh no! After what Mr. Jamieson said, I'm afraid to ask Papa what he's heard. Then again, I need to know.

"What have you heard?"

Papa pauses before he answers. "Some people think that a group home for teenagers is needed in the area. They don't have a problem with it being opened in our neighborhood," he says. "But other people are certain that they do not want it here."

Once again the heat starts building inside me.

"I can't believe people are so mean!" Suddenly I can't eat any more chicken and rice.

Papa nods, then he tries to change the subject. "Have you heard from your mom lately?"

"*Oui*," I say.

"Have you phoned or texted her back?"

I can't sit here any longer. I stand up and take my plate to the dishwasher.

"*Non*. Maman made her choice." I blink back tears. "I'm going to my room. I have more knitting to do and some homework."

Papa scratches his beard. "Okay, *chérie*. But the hockey game is on soon, if you would like to join me."

My dad is a lifelong fan of the Montreal Canadiens. I sometimes watch the games with him. My mother never did. I think again about how she became a hockey fan as soon as she moved in with Zoltan. My jaw clenches into a knot.

When I get to my room, I text Amira, Dionne and Liam.

Hey guys. How's the knitting going?

Within minutes all three have replied. Each of them has almost finished a scarf. Counting the two scarves I've already made, we just need one more.

I remember something. I reach into the back of my closet and pull out a bag. Inside is a beige scarf. Knitting needles and a ball of yarn are still attached to it. The scarf has a stitch running down the middle called a cable.

It looks like a twisted rope. In Ireland especially, people started working this cable pattern into the sweaters and scarves they knit for their loved ones who worked out at sea. The cable is a symbol of the rope they hope will guide them safely home. I thought that was a cool story, so I started making a cable scarf for my mom. It was supposed to be for her birthday next month. But after she moved away to be with Zoltan, I tucked it away.

I glance over at the homework I'm supposed to do tonight. I have some math problems and a short English essay to write. But the scarf just needs another eight or twelve rows.

I sit down and quickly finish it. As I'm casting off the last stitches, another text comes through. I glance at my phone in case it's my friends again. But it's from my mother.

"Quel dommage, Maman," I mutter. What a shame. She's missing out on a nice scarf.

Chapter Six

The first kid I meet from the group home is Jude. He turns up in my drama class. For the first few days he sits at the back of the room, his dark curls covering most of his face. Our class is pretty small. It isn't long before Mr. Silva pairs us up for a drama exercise. We have to tell a story where each of us adds one word at a time.

Before Jude can say anything, I start. "The…"

He jumps right in. "Speckled."

"Dinosaur."

"Smiled," he says.

"Are you sure speckled dinosaurs smile?" I ask.

"Sure," Jude answers. "Why not?"

By the time we finish our story, the speckled dinosaur has sailed on a pirate ship, gone snowboarding, adopted a pet snake and is getting a neck tattoo. The other groups are still creating their stories. While we wait for them to finish, I tell Jude about the volunteer work the Unity Club does around the city.

"I don't know if you're interested," I say, "but we're always happy to get new members."

Jude doesn't answer. But he's looking at me intensely with his dark eyes.

I feel my face flushing. I swallow hard and try to sound casual. "Then again,"

I say, "I know you're just getting settled in and stuff."

I told the Unity Club members not to pressure the new students, but I realize I may have just done that to Jude. I also realize he's pretty cute.

"There's something else I want to tell you," I say. "The people in our club made something for everyone living at the—"

Will I embarrass him if I mention the group home?

"At the group home." Jude's voice is soft.

"Yeah," I say. "We made a welcome gift for each of you. And we stored them here in the drama room. This is where the Unity Club meets. If you'd like, I could give you the box later. Or I could drop it off—at the house."

I feel a pang as I picture hanging out there with my mom. Just then Mr. Silva calls the class back together.

"Do you want to meet here after school?" Jude asks.

"Sure. I'll give you the box then."

As promised, Jude is waiting for me in the drama room. We end up walking home together. Jude carries the box of scarves. When we reach the Blue House—which is what I've decided to call it—I don't say anything about how I used to live here.

Before I leave, I mention the club once again. "If you'd like to find out more, there's an open house at the school on Wednesday. It's mainly for elementary students who are thinking about coming to Addison next year. But the Unity Club is setting up a display. You might find it interesting."

"I'll think about it," Jude says. "Thanks again. I'll make sure everyone gets their gift tonight." He heads into the Blue House.

Later that night I start to wonder who got the cable-knit scarf. That's totally

out of my hands. Still, I secretly hope
Jude ended up with it.

Chapter Seven

Amira has printed out some pamphlets about the Unity Club. She is stacking them in a neat pile at our booth at the open house. Meanwhile, the cross-country running team, photography club, chess club and Rubik's Cubers are all setting up in their spots down the hall from us.

The principal's opening talk in the gym has ended. It's getting busier around the club displays. I'm chatting with some parents and nervous elementary-school kids who are thinking about coming to Addison near year. Just then, Jude walks down the hallway. He stops to talk to Liam and Eliza.

Once the crowds clear, Liam turns to me. "Hey, Brett! I think we have our newest Unity Club member here."

"I'm not sure yet." Jude laughs. "I'm still figuring stuff out at—"

"At the Blue House?" I say.

Jude looks relieved. "Yeah, at the Blue House. I don't know all the rules yet about off-site activities. I'll check and let you know. I can text you later if you want, Brett."

"Sure thing." As we put our numbers into each other's phones, I'm trying hard not to blush.

Just then a loud voice rings out. "We were thinking of sending Mia to Addison next year. But now we probably won't."

Everyone looks over at a woman who is shaking her head as she scans the booths. She seems to want everyone to hear her. A teen girl is shuffling beside her, hands shoved deep in her pockets.

"Why not, Jayne?" The woman beside her looks up from her phone. "Isn't this the closest middle school for you?"

"Yes, but I'm not impressed by that group home that went in down the street," the woman says.

Another parent joins in. "I heard a bunch of the kids from the group home are students here," he says. "I bet the school is busy dealing with lots of behavioral issues now. I wonder how much *learning* is actually going on here."

Every muscle in my body tenses up. I can't believe that grown adults are talking like this. I glance over at Jude. His head is down. He probably wishes the ground would open up and swallow him.

"The problems in the neighborhood have already started," the man says. "Mr. Giovanni's fence got knocked over the other night."

"Yes, and the fence had already been covered in graffiti," someone else chimes in.

"I think this is just the start of our problems with that place."

Unfortunately, I recognize the last voice. It's Mr. Jamieson. And now he has found other people with the same bad attitude. I glance to my right and see that Jude has slipped away. I feel like doing the same thing. I need to get away from these people and their nasty comments.

I pull out my phone to check the time. As I'm doing that a text comes through.

Bonjour, chérie. **Are you getting my texts?**

Maman! I grit my teeth and stuff my phone back into my pocket.

"It's time to pack up." I say it louder than necessary. I hope everyone will move on. Thankfully, they do.

Amira turns to me as we take down the display boards. "I can't believe those people," she says.

"Me either." I drop the pamphlets into a box.

"And why did they say those things right in front of Jude?" Eliza says. "That was so mean."

"I know," I say. "Even if there *has* been some damage in the neighborhood, they have no proof the kids from the group home did it."

"I hate to say it," Liam says, "but the timing is pretty suspicious."

I glance over at Kaden. Given how negative he has been lately, I'm bracing myself for what he might say.

"That doesn't mean anything," Kaden says. "Stuff like that happens all the time."

Wow, he is full of surprises.

"I'm with Kaden." I smile and try to make eye contact with him. But he looks away. We pick up the boxes and lug everything down the hall to store in the drama room.

I think about what Mike told me about NIMBY—*not in my backyard*. I had hoped this kind of negativity about the group home wouldn't happen, yet it has. But I won't let it carry over into the Unity Club. No way.

After the open house, the group decides to meet up at our neighborhood coffee shop, Beans Bistro. I'm surprised when Kaden joins us.

"We so earned our hot chocolates tonight," Amira says as we grab some chairs and wedge them around a table.

I'm still burning about what those parents said at the school, so I mostly let everyone else do the talking. Suddenly a loud voice from the far corner of the shop catches everyone's attention.

Jude is sitting at that table with a guy who looks a few years older than him. The guy is flailing his arms and speaking so loudly that nobody can miss what he's saying.

"Nobody gets to tell me where I can—"

Jude is trying to shush him. "Ricardo, keep it down."

"He owes me money." Ricardo pounds his fist on the table. "He promised me I'd get it this week!" Then he gets up and storms out the door.

The coffee shop has fallen silent. Everyone is looking at Jude. He picks up both coffee cups.

"Sorry about that," he says to the woman behind the counter as he hands her the cups.

Jude wasn't the one doing the yelling, so it was nice of him to apologize. As he's heading toward the door, he sees our table. He pauses as though he can't decide whether to stop and talk to us.

"Hey," Kaden says. "Don't you have curfews or something?"

The kind thoughts I'd had earlier for Kaden vanish. Jude turns and walks out the door without a word.

"Why did you say that?" I ask.

"Yeah," Amira says. "Jude was already embarrassed."

"I didn't mean anything by it." Kaden shrugs his shoulders. "I'm just pretty sure they have curfews in group homes. I mean, I think they do."

As for me, I've had enough. Despite the positive example I've tried to set,

I realize it's happened. Negative thoughts about the Blue House and the teens who live there have crept into the Unity Club.

I need to do something to counter them before things get any worse.

Chapter Eight

When I get home, I open the Unity Club's Facebook page. I need to post a group message.

I think back to when the grumbling about the group home began. It was the day I met Mike at the Blue House. At least, that's when I first heard Mr. Jamieson complain about it. I haven't seen Mike since then, but I remember what he told me.

I start writing my post. I explain what NIMBY means. I give examples of how people often agree that things like landfill sites or women's shelters are necessary, but then they complain if those things are built in their neighborhoods. I point out the importance of supporting all members of our community. I finish by saying I feel the Unity Club has a duty to set a strong example by supporting the group home.

The comments that the club members make on the post over the next few days are positive. That's a huge relief. But it bothers me that I haven't seen Jude lately. Maybe he's still upset about the horrible things people said at the open house. And Kaden was so rude to him at the coffee shop—right in front of the rest of the Unity Club. I wonder if Jude thinks we all look down on him because he lives in the Blue House.

When I see Jude leaving school the next day, I call out to him. At first, he just keeps walking. Then he slows down and waits for me.

"I was going to text you," I say as we trudge through the snow. "But then I decided to wait. Because I wanted to say something to you in person."

Jude glances sideways at me. "What's that?"

I take a deep breath. "I'm sorry about what Kaden said to you at the coffee shop. You know, about curfews."

Jude doesn't say anything.

"That was really rude of him," I say. "I wish I'd spoken up right there and told him that. But he caught me by surprise."

Jude nods, a slow smile crossing his face. "Thanks," he says. "You know, we actually *do* have curfews at the Blue House. And there are a lot of rules. But I guess we need some rules. Some of us do, at least…"

Jude trails off. I wait to see if he is going to say anything else. He doesn't. But I think he has accepted my apology. I decide to change the subject.

"Remember you said you might be interested in joining the Unity Club?" I say. "We could really use some extra volunteers tomorrow at Mini Gym Kids. We catch the city bus outside our school at four o'clock. Then we go downtown and play games with the kids at Lennox School."

Jude smiles. "Lennox was one of my old schools," he says. "It was my fourth school." He tilts his head. "Or maybe my fifth. I can't remember. I've changed schools a lot since I moved here from Haiti."

"Haiti? Cool," I say. "And hopefully you'll get to stay here." I feel a familiar heat spreading across my face. I clear my throat to try to cover up. "And it'd be great if you come with us on Tuesday," I say. "You know, so you can get to know some more people."

Even as I say that, I know it's not just about Jude meeting new people. It's about me getting to hang out with him too.

"What time does it end?" Jude asks.

"We're usually back by around six o'clock," I say.

Jude nods. "That would work," he says. "I have to check in at the Blue House sometime after school. But as long as I do that by seven, it's all okay."

"That's pretty much what I have to do with my dad too," I say.

"What about your mom?" Jude asks.

I shake my head. "She doesn't live with us anymore."

As if on cue, my phone vibrates. I give it a quick glance.

"Speak of the devil," I say.

"The devil?" Jude laughs. "She can't be that bad."

I decide it's better not to say anything. Before I know it, we're at the group home.

"I'll see you tomorrow," Jude says.

"Yeah," I say. "See you."

I only pause for a moment to watch as Jude walks into my mom's old house and closes the door behind him.

The next day I'm shivering at the bus stop with the other volunteers when Jude steps out of the school. He races toward us. I smile when I notice he's wearing the beige scarf with the cable.

We all pile onto the bus, and before long we're downtown. Including the new grade-one students, over two dozen little kids are waiting for us. A roar goes up the moment we step into the gym.

"So who's going to have fun today?" Cohen calls out.

"Me!"

"Me!"

"I will!"

Their cute little-kid voices echo around us.

"Today," Eliza says, "we have some new people to play with. Can all the grade-one students raise their hands?"

About ten hands shoot into the air.

"Let's all take a look at our new grade-one friends," Eliza says. "These new buddies are a little bit smaller than everyone else. That means we're going to be extra careful today to make sure they all get turns. Does that sound fair?"

Many of the kids jump up and down as they call out in agreement.

"Good," Eliza says. "And now there's someone else I need to introduce. A new big buddy has joined us today. Can everyone say hi to Jude?"

Eliza points at Jude. He looks surprised but then he smiles and waves at the little kids.

"Hi!"

"Hi!"

"Hi, Jude!" They cry as they wave back at him.

When the gym is quiet again, Cohen speaks up. "Does anyone have a favorite game they'd like to play today?"

"Dodgeball! Dodgeball!" Everyone shouts at the same time.

"We played that last week," Liam says. "Let's ask our new grade-one friends what game they'd like to play."

"Dodgeball! Dodgeball!" they shout.

"Okay," Cohen says. "I guess we're playing dodgeball. Remember, we're not going to throw the ball too hard. We don't want anyone to get hurt. And if you get hit, you have to go wait at the side of the gym for one minute. Then you get to come back in."

Eliza and Amira divide the students into two teams. Each team has three Unity Club members on it too. Before long the ball is bouncing around the gym.

Nora, a little girl in grade one, has attached herself to me. She gives me a sad look when the ball hits her leg. "That's okay, Nora," I say. "I'll go sit out for you." I cheer her on from the sidelines.

Our crew moves among the little kids. They hand the ball to the ones who haven't had turns yet. Kids are laughing and bouncing all over the place. The excitement ramps up even more as Jude somersaults and flops to keep from getting hit. The little kids howl with laughter at Jude's goofy stunts.

"Here, Cooper." I hand the ball to a quiet little boy with big square glasses. "I bet you'll get Jude out!"

Cooper gives me a quiet smile and throws the ball. When it hardly dribbles past the center line, I get it and hand it back to him. "Try again," I say. "You'll get him this time!"

His next throw isn't much better. But as it rolls to the other side of the gym, Jude pretends to trip. He flops onto the gym floor so that the ball touches his foot. A cheer goes up around the gym for Cooper, who pumps both fists into the air.

When our gym time ends, the little kids give us waves, fist bumps and high fives. Then we make our way outside to the bus stop.

"That was fun," Cohen says as we ride back to school.

"It totally was." Amira turns to Jude. "Great dodgeball moves!"

Jude's smile is almost as big as Cooper's was. "Thanks," he says. "Cooper is a pretty cool kid!"

The streetlamps are coming on just as we're getting off the bus. As we pass the seniors' residence, Liam comes to a stop and points.

"Oh no!" he says.

Chapter Nine

We all gasp when we see the bench.
The Unity Club raised funds to buy it
last year. It was practically brand-new.
But now it is tipped backward into the
snow. Its metal frame is twisted, and the
wooden slats are broken.

We're still looking at it when a police
cruiser passes by. Ever since the group
home went in, I've noticed the police

doing more regular checks through the neighborhood. I wave to flag them down.

The police car pulls up alongside us. A female officer is the first to step out of it.

"Did any of you see what happened?" she asks.

Nobody says anything right away. It occurs to me that maybe she thinks we're responsible for this. A group of kids out after dark. I decide to speak up.

"No," I say. "We just got off the city bus. We were all volunteering downtown. The bench wasn't like this when we left."

"Yeah," Liam says. "We would have noticed."

The entire group still looks shocked. But when my eyes land on Jude, I see something else on his face. Fear. That's weird. He was with the rest of the Unity

Club when this happened. He definitely had nothing to do with it.

The officer's words interrupt my thoughts. "What time did you leave to go downtown?"

"We left here at four o'clock," Amira says.

The officer checks her watch. "So this happened between four o'clock and six o'clock?"

"It must have, yes," I say.

Some people from the neighborhood are gathering to see what's going on.

"If I were you, I'd go talk to the kids at the new group home." A man tugs on the dog leash in his hand. "This sort of nonsense started right after that group home opened up down the street."

The heat is rising within me. I suddenly notice Jude isn't here.

"Jude left a few minutes ago," Amira whispers.

I'm not thrilled that she figured out who I was looking for. But right now, I need to get out of here before I say something I'll regret.

"Who would destroy our bench like that?" Amira asks as we head home. "We spent months fundraising to buy it. Now the seniors from Fairview Court will have nowhere to sit while they wait for the bus."

"I know," I say. "I have no idea who would do such a thing."

Under the streetlamps, I see Amira biting the side of her lip.

"Do you think it's possible," she finally says, "that some of the kids from the group home might have—"

Before I can stop them, the words are out of my mouth. "Not you too! People are blaming them for everything. It's totally unfair." I realize my voice is louder than I intended.

"Okay, you don't have to bite my head off. I was just asking."

We walk the rest of the way in silence, past the Blue House. When we get to the turnoff to Amira's house, she walks away without saying another word.

Does this qualify as my first fight with my best friend? Do I need to text her and say I'm sorry?

It feels like all the air got sucked out of my lungs. I slog the rest of the way home through the snow.

The next day, our principal calls a school assembly. Everyone is usually pretty rowdy when all the students get together in the gym like this. But today the serious look on Ms. Chen's face keeps everyone quiet.

"As you know," she says, "I don't usually call an assembly for the whole school. I dislike interrupting our instructional time. But this seems rather an unusual situation."

She pushes her bright-yellow glasses back up on her nose. "Our staff and our students work hard to create a positive environment at Addison Junior High School. But recently we have had a number of incidents of vandalism. Earlier this week a window was smashed. That was the third broken window in two weeks. We've also had to power-wash graffiti off the brick wall out behind the school. And, as some of you know, the bench that our Unity Club bought and donated to the seniors at Fairview Court was destroyed last night."

Angry murmurs ripple through the gym.

I see Amira sitting two rows ahead of me. She didn't meet me this morning to walk to school. She also didn't find me before the assembly so we could sit together. Then again, I didn't go find her either. I still don't know if she's angry with me or not.

"I've spoken with the police," Ms. Chen continues. "I don't believe they have any leads so far. As you know, many of the seniors at Fairview can no longer drive. They rely on the bus to get to their appointments. And I am pretty sure that when I am seventy-five or eighty years old, I would like a bench to sit on while I wait for the bus."

The mention of the seniors gives me a pang of guilt. I realize I haven't even checked in with Mrs. Rashid to see if she's feeling better.

"This particular act of vandalism did not occur right on Addison school grounds. Still, the bench was a gift from our students. And those seniors are an important part of our community." Ms. Chen frowns. "This is why I brought everybody here today. In situations like this, someone often knows who was responsible. If you have any information, I ask that you come and talk to me privately."

A silence has fallen over the gym. I take another look around, and my gaze lands on Jude. He is sitting near the back of the gym, beside Brady. Brady has been a student here for a few years now. He has a reputation for having an explosive temper. I wish Jude was sitting with somebody else. I also wonder about the guy Jude was with at the coffee shop the other night. And why did Jude slip away last night as soon as the police arrived?

Ms. Chen's words interrupt my thoughts. "Before I close the assembly, I want to be clear on one final point," she says. "When problems like these occur, it's easy for people to start pointing fingers. And for people to start accusing others without having any facts to back them up. The last thing I want is for people to turn against other groups within our school or within our community. We need to address this situation together. And we need to do it respectfully."

It feels like a weight lifts from my shoulders when Ms. Chen says that last part. But then my hopes crash back down—because in the buzz of voices around me, I can hear that students are blaming the kids from the group home. It's already happening.

Amira glances back my way as everyone is leaving the gym. I start to smile at her, thinking she might wait up for me. But she looks away and continues out into the hall. I swallow a lump in my throat. My job as president of the Unity Club just became more complicated. And not nearly as much fun.

Chapter Ten

Jude isn't in the drama room after school. I delay starting the meeting for as long as I can. I keep hoping he'll show up. I pretend to be busy shuffling through some supplies at the back of the room. Amira is doing her best to avoid looking at me the entire time.

"Is this meeting ever gonna happen?" Georgia says.

My stomach twists into a knot. I go and join the group. "I guess we'd better get started," I say. "First of all, we had a really good turnout for Mini Gym Kids last night. But we could still use more volunteers, especially now that the grade-one students are participating too."

I know I need to mention the damaged bench, but I can't do it yet.

"Fairview Court is still shut down because of the flu outbreak," I say instead. "But they have probably given the blankets to the new senior citizens who live there by now."

"They have for sure," Kaden says.

Given how rarely Kaden says anything, everyone turns and stares.

"My grandmother moved there six weeks ago," Kaden explains. "She loves her new blanket. She couldn't believe at first that it was hers to keep."

"That's so sweet," Amira says.

Kaden nods. "One of the residents had a stroke a while back. Since then he hasn't been able to use the left side of his body very much. But Gran said he kept smiling and touching the blanket—with his left hand."

I'm staring at Kaden. I can hardly believe he just shared that with the group. Is this really the same guy who has been surly and difficult the past few months? For a moment, I get a glimpse of what a good Unity Club president he might have made.

"That's amazing, Kaden," I say.

"Yeah, thanks for telling us." Amira's eyes are filled with tears.

I'm about to smile at Amira, but I stop myself. Are we still friends or not? She turns away, so I guess we aren't.

"And the last thing," I try to keep my voice steady, "is the scarves we knit for the group-home kids. I sent them over there with Jude. I'm sure they appreciate them."

"They'd better," Georgia mutters.

"Yeah," Suresh says. "After what they did to our bench."

My face burns. Many of the students are nodding. It's time for me to address this.

I take a deep breath. "We need to talk about the bench," I say. "I get that everyone is upset. I'm really sad too for our friends at the seniors' home. Maybe we can talk about launching another fundraiser for a new—"

"You've got to be kidding!" Tassie interrupts. "I don't have the heart to do more bake sales and bottle drives."

"Me either," Eliza says. "And I don't care what Ms. Chen said at the assembly. I think we all know who wrecked our bench."

"Absolutely," Suresh says. "None of this stuff was happening until the group home went in."

It suddenly feels like someone cranked up the heat in the room. I'm fighting to keep my voice even.

"Look," I say. "We don't have to decide right now about fundraising for another bench. We can talk about it again after the shock has worn off. When we can look at it more objectively."

"Objectively?" Georgia's hands wave through the air as she speaks. "There's nothing to be objective *about*."

"Exactly," Suresh says. "The bench that we worked so hard for was ruined."

"It was stupid and senseless," Eliza says. "The seniors *need* that bench."

"I agree. I'm just saying—"

"I think what you're saying," Suresh says, "is that you're too busy welcoming the group-home kids to our school to notice the obvious problem."

I try to stay calm. "Like I said, I think it's best if we wait and talk about the bench after everyone has cooled down."

Whenever I look at anyone, they immediately look away. It's clear they don't want to listen to what I have to say. And it's clear that everyone is questioning my leadership of the Unity Club.

But then I notice there is *one* person who doesn't look away when my eyes land on him. Surprisingly, that person is Kaden.

Since no one is talking, I speak up again. "I guess we'll wrap up the meeting early today. And I think we need to remember what Ms. Chen said about not pointing fingers at anyone." I take another deep breath. "Let's remember too that the Unity Club made an official decision to welcome the new students from the group home. It's still up to us to set an example for everyone else."

I stand up to indicate the meeting has ended. I usually hang around after the meetings in case anyone wants to chat. But today I'm the first to leave.

I'm almost out the door when Justine speaks up. "That official decision she's talking about? I think it has more to do with a certain guy she likes than anything else."

"Yeah," Suresh says. "Our president definitely has a crush on Jude."

I realize there's some truth to this. I *do* like Jude. He's fun and he's cute. But the club decided to support the group home before I'd even met Jude. So those comments are unfair too.

Suddenly I can't get out of the school fast enough.

Chapter Eleven

The kitchen smells like chimichurri sauce when I get home from school. We ate it in our chicken-and-rice concoction the past two nights. Sure enough, the saucepan with the bright-green sauce is still soaking in the sink. Neither Papa nor I had time to wash it last night.

I'm starting to chop our usual veggies and chicken when I realize

I can't do it. I can't eat another one of those dinners.

I rummage through the fridge. I pull out the eggs and milk, and I check the crisper for vegetables. Red peppers, onions and some tired-looking spinach from the salad we never got around to making. I find a frozen pie shell at the back of the freezer. Maman would have no problem turning this into something fantastic. Probably one of her amazing quiches. Tonight, I decide, I'm going to do the same. Or at least I'm going to try.

I search online for recipes. Some of them have ingredients similar to what we have on hand. I choose one and start prepping. I add extra red peppers and spinach to make up for the asparagus it calls for. I grate cheddar cheese because we don't have any Swiss.

It takes me forever because I have to keep checking the recipe on my phone. That makes it harder to avoid my mom's texts. Since Maman has quiche down to a fine art, I could just ask her how to do this. But there's no way I'm letting her know that I need her or her help.

I fish the last of the eggshells out of the bowl. Then I beat the eggs and pour them into the pie shell. I pop the whole jiggly mess into the oven and cross my fingers. I've just finished cleaning up when Papa comes in.

"*Bonjour, chérie*," he says. "Something smells good!"

"*Bonjour*, Papa. I didn't hear you pull up."

"I'm not surprised," he says, peering into the oven. "Because you've been busy cooking—"

"Quiche," I say. "At least, I hope it's going to be quiche. I thought it was time for a change."

"I see," Papa says with a smile. "Did you phone your mom for the recipe?" He sounds hopeful.

"*Non!* I pulled up a recipe on the Internet."

My phone vibrates on the counter just as the oven timer goes off. My dad can see it's a text from Maman.

"Aren't you going to answer that?" he asks.

"*Pas maintenant*," I say. Not now.

Papa sighs and runs his hand across his face.

"Long day?" I ask.

"*Oui.* And I have to go back to the office again tonight. I just came home to see you and to eat a quick dinner. Sorry, *chérie*."

"That's okay," I say. "I have lots of homework tonight anyway."

Papa plops down onto one of the kitchen chairs. I put the quiche on the table and slice into it. It seems kind of rubbery, but it smells fantastic. I load up our plates.

"So, tell me what you've been up to," Papa says.

I take a few bites. Then I tell him everything that's happened in the last twenty-four hours.

"And now," I finish, "everyone in the Unity Club thinks they know who's responsible for the bench and for the other damage around the neighborhood. They think it's the people living in the group home. Even though they don't have any proof."

We both are quiet for a bit.

"What about you?" I ask. "Have you heard anything?"

"*Oui*," Papa says. "I'm hearing the same. Many people think the kids from the group home are causing the problems."

I slam my fork down onto the table. "Everyone is so quick to blame them," I say. "But nobody knows for sure."

Papa keeps eating his quiche, not saying anything.

"I mean, I know it looks bad," I say. "Many of the problems started *after* the group home went in. But even the people who supported the group home in the beginning are turning on them."

I don't mention that even my best friends—actually, my *former* best friends—are doing that. Papa still doesn't say anything.

"These are people who would normally be in favor of a group home for teenagers," I say. "As long as—"

"As long as it was not right in their backyard." Papa runs his hand through his hair so many times that it sticks up. "There are no easy answers, Brett. Those teenagers need to live somewhere. I just hope this is the right place for them."

"What do you mean?" After what happened with the Unity Club

members, Papa's words have me bristling with anger. "Why wouldn't it be the right place for them?"

"I don't know how the group home is being run," Papa says. "Or whether the teens living there are the ones who are best suited to it. *Je ne sais pas*."

"I don't know either," I say. "But I think people need to be kinder and more open-minded."

Papa nods and finishes his dinner. "Brett, that was delicious. *Merci*." He puts his plate and cutlery into the dishwasher. "It was at least as good as your mom's."

"That's maybe pushing it," I say. "But yeah, it was pretty good."

Papa smiles and plants a kiss on the top of my head. "Are you okay if I head back to the office now? I'll try not to be too late."

"Okay, Papa."

While I finish my last few bites, I scroll through the texts from my mom.

Her new job, her new co-workers, her plans for the weekend with Zoltan. Nothing I want to hear about.

I pull out my homework and sigh. After the day I've had, I don't really want to talk to anyone. But I also don't want to be alone.

I pack up my things, layer up and hurry outside into the cold.

Chapter Twelve

I've got my homework spread across a table at Beans Bistro, and I'm sipping my hot chocolate. The conversation between two women at the next table is making me wish I'd stayed at home.

"All this vandalism around town—it wouldn't have happened if it weren't for that group home."

"They should just shut it down, if you ask me."

Except that nobody asked you. Jeez, can't people find something else to talk about? I'm relieved when the women finish their coffee and leave.

I turn back to the lab report I have to finish. I'm nearly done when Jude walks in. He's with the same guy I saw him with here last time.

Jude waves as he walks by. I notice he's wearing the cable scarf again. I think back to how mean everyone was at the last meeting and their comments about Jude. I'm sure glad I didn't tell anyone about the special scarf I added to the box.

I'm closing my binder when the older boy walks out of the coffee shop. Instead of leaving with him, Jude comes over to my table.

"Don't tell me," he says. "You're doing your science, right?"

"Yeah," I say. "Did you get yours done?"

"Not yet," he says. "But I don't have that class tomorrow. I still have time."

He stands there shuffling his feet.

"Do you want to sit down?"

"Sure." Jude swings into the chair across from me. "This is a good place," he says. "I like it here."

"Me too," I say. "We're lucky to have this coffee shop right in the neighborhood."

"So have you always lived in Edmonton?" he asks.

"Yes. And I remember you saying you were born in Haiti. What was it like there?"

"I don't remember much about it," he replies. "I was pretty young when we moved to Canada. My parents loved Haiti. But natural disasters kept happening. Massive earthquakes. Flooding. My folks finally decided we had to leave."

"That must have been really hard for them," I say.

Jude doesn't say anything. It starts to feel a little too quiet at our table, so I start telling Jude about my family.

"It's just me and my dad at my place," I say. "I'm an only child, and my parents got divorced a few years ago. My mom moved to Winnipeg a while back. She wanted to be closer to her new boyfriend."

I don't realize there's an edge in my voice until Jude speaks up. "So I'm guessing you don't like him very much."

"I've never met the guy," I say. "But—"

Jude's phone vibrates. He looks at it, then jumps up from the table.

"Sorry," he says. "I need to go."

"Is everything okay?"

But he dashes from the coffee shop without another word. I don't think he even heard me.

I pack up my homework and pull on my coat. I think about our conversation as I head back out into the cold. I probably shouldn't have complained to Jude about my mom. His situation is probably way worse than mine. Otherwise, he wouldn't be living in a group home. Still, he was easy to talk to. And he seemed to really listen to me. At least until that text came through.

An ambulance zips by, its siren blaring.

"Oh no!" I cry as I see it stop in front of the seniors' home.

I start running.

A few of the residents from the seniors' home braved the cold to get out for an evening walk. They are hovering between the sidewalk and the entrance. I weave through them to try to find out what is happening.

As I get closer, I see someone lying crumpled on the ground. I watch the ambulance attendants lift the person onto a stretcher. I can see in the light from the streetlamp that it's an elderly woman. A third paramedic is talking to an aide from the seniors' home.

"My shift was over, and I was just leaving." The aide wipes away tears. "When I came outside, there she was, lying on the ground."

"Was anyone here with her?" the attendant asks.

"I don't think so." She shakes her head. "Some teenagers were across the street, but I didn't really pay any attention to them. I was too worried about getting her in out of the cold." The aide wrings her hands. "But I was afraid to move her in case she'd broken something. I phoned the ambulance right away."

As the other two attendants lift the stretcher into the back of the ambulance,

I get a glimpse of the woman's face. It's Mrs. Rashid! Her eyes are closed, and her features are pinched.

Oh no, oh no, oh no! Mrs. Rashid was already weak from the flu. And now this?

As the ambulance pulls away, people start to leave. But I can't move. I don't know how long I stand there before I realize I'm shivering. The chill starts somewhere in my boots and works its way up. I can't stop my teeth from chattering.

I cross my arms against my chest and start walking home. I'm at the far end of the seniors' home when something in the snow catches my eye.

As I get closer, I see a scarf—with a cable pattern running through it. My blood runs even colder. Why is Jude's scarf here?

I snap it up and hurry home.

Chapter Thirteen

I hardly sleep that night. I keep thinking about Mrs. Rashid. I feel sick when I picture how frail and broken she looked.

In the morning, I haul myself out of bed and check my phone. There's still nothing from Amira. But, of course, my mom has sent me a bunch of texts. About Zoltan's kids not accepting her and being difficult when she's around.

How she's thinking about getting her own apartment in Winnipeg.

If she expects any sympathy from me, she can forget it. Plus, I have other things on my mind. Like, how my dad learned from a friend in the neighborhood last night that Mrs. Rashid broke her hip. She's going to need surgery. What if—

No, I can't even finish that thought. I hurry to get ready, then head off for school. Soon that feels like a mistake. The moment I step inside the school, I can tell word has gotten around about Mrs. Rashid's fall. I look for Jude, but there's no sign of him today. Or any of the other kids from the group home. After what happened last night, their absence doesn't look good at all.

Wow. I realize I'm starting to think like everybody else. Maybe there's a perfectly good reason why they're not here. Maybe they decided there was no point coming to school, since everyone thinks they're guilty anyway. I would have trouble showing up if it were me.

I'm trying not to jump to conclusions, but I'm furious at all of them. At Jude especially. Until now I never doubted myself when I said the Unity Club needed to welcome the teens from the group home. But after what happened to Mrs. Rashid, I wonder if maybe I was wrong. Maybe the scarf stuffed into the bottom of my backpack is proof. All I know is, I need some answers.

By the end of the day, I'm so stressed that I can't wait to leave school. I just need to get away from it all. Then I remember that the Unity Club has a meeting. Amira still isn't talking to me or I'd send her a message saying I can't make it. That I have an appointment or something. But since that's not an option, I head to the drama room to deliver the message myself.

I'm nearly there when I bump into Kaden. He's one of the last people I want to see right now. Suddenly all my frustration and worry bubble up to the surface.

"You know you owe Jude an apology, right?" The words are out of my mouth before I can stop them. "For what you said to him at Beans, about needing to leave because of his curfew?"

Kaden just stands there, his eyes wide and his mouth open.

"Sorry," he says finally. "I guess I don't always think before I—"

I don't give him a chance to finish. "And since you seem to think you would be a better president than me," I say, "you can lead the meeting today."

I turn and leave before Kaden can say anything else.

I trudge through the snow to the Blue House and knock on the door.

While I'm waiting for someone to answer, I start peeling off some layers.

I've just stuffed my gloves inside my backpack when Jude opens the door.

"Oh, hey." He glances back over his shoulder. "Um, I'm not allowed to bring visitors inside," he says. "It's one of the rules."

"Fine," I say. "Grab a coat. I'll wait for you out here."

Jude closes the door. I sit down on the porch. When my mom lived here, she had comfy furniture out here that looked like it was made from tree branches. We spent hours reading on the big, overstuffed cushions. Now there's just a couch and some wooden chairs shoved into a corner.

I'm perched on the edge of the hard vinyl couch when Jude appears, wearing his coat and running shoes.

"Did you forget your scarf?" I ask.

Jude looks puzzled, but he doesn't answer. "Sorry I can't invite you inside." He sits down beside me.

"It's okay," I say. "I actually know this house well. It was my mom's house until she moved to Winnipeg."

"Really? Your mom lived here?"

"Yeah," I say. "Until she ditched me to be in Winnipeg with her new boyfriend."

Right on cue, my phone buzzes. "That's probably her now," I say.

"Aren't you going to answer?" Jude asks.

Something about the way he says that makes me grit my teeth. It's as though he thinks I *should* text her back.

"No." I take a deep breath. "She could have stuck around, but she chose not to."

At least I'm angry enough now to tell Jude why I really came here.

"You probably heard Mrs. Rashid got hurt last night outside Fairview Court. They took her away in an ambulance."

Jude nods. "Yeah, I heard that," he says. "Is she going to be okay?"

"I don't know." My voice shakes. "She broke her hip, and she needs to have surgery. She's eighty-four. This surgery will be hard on her." Then I turn toward Jude and stare at him hard. "Some teenagers were nearby when it happened. So I need to know if…"

"You need to know if I pushed her or something?"

I can't hold his gaze. I just look down at my boots and nod.

"No," Jude says. "I didn't do anything. But I was there when—"

Just then someone comes out the front door. It's Mike, the guy who first told me about the group home. He looks over at us sitting together.

"You know the rules, Jude. No guests." Mike runs his hands across his face. "As you know, I've got enough on my plate. Trying to keep track of everyone and make sure they respect the rules and curfews…" He shakes his head as his voice trails off.

Mike goes back inside. But I can see him watching us from the front window.

"Look," Jude says. "I was across the street when Mrs. Rashid fell. I was going over to see if I could help her. But then a woman who works there came out the front door. I saw her go to Mrs. Rashid. Then she made a phone call. So I left."

"You just left?" My hands are waving as I speak.

Jude's face reddens. "Yes," he says. "But only after I saw she had help. After what happened with the bench, I knew it would look bad on me and the others from the group home if I was seen there." Jude's eyes lock onto mine. "I need you to believe me, Brett. I would not hurt Mrs. Rashid—or anyone else."

I think back to how much fun Jude was at Mini Gym Kids. And I remember how easy it was to talk to him about my mom moving away. I want to believe him, but I'm not sure what to think anymore.

I reach into my backpack. "I think you dropped this last night." I hand him the scarf. "I found it outside Fairview Court."

"Thanks," he says as he takes it from me.

"Are you coming back to school tomorrow?" I ask.

"I'm not sure that's a good idea. It was bad enough when it was just vandalism and stuff happening around the school. But now?" Jude runs his hands through his hair. "Actually, Brett, I'm probably going to change schools."

My stomach knots up. "You can't just leave."

The moment the words are out of my mouth, I realize how ridiculous I sound. Jude can do whatever he wants to. Or, at least, I think he can.

Right now I need some time to try and figure this out. I'm partway down the porch stairs when Jude calls out.

"Brett?" he says. "I get that you're mad at your mom. But you need to text her back."

"Really?" I come to a full stop. "You're planning to run away from your problems. But you think you can give me advice about how to deal with my mom?"

Mike opens the front door. Before he can tell me again to leave, I stomp away as fast as I can.

Chapter Fourteen

Jude doesn't come to school for the rest of the week. I think about texting him to see if he's already switched schools. I could say I'm asking because we still need more people at Mini Gym Kids. But I can't bring myself to do it. I'm still stinging about him telling me I should talk to my mom. And even though I want to believe him when he said he had nothing to do with Mrs. Rashid's accident, I still have doubts.

There's a Unity Club meeting after school today. I have no idea how I'm going to handle that one. Everyone is still talking about Mrs. Rashid's accident. And they're still barely looking at me. Plus, they're questioning my leadership, especially after I missed the last meeting. The fun has been sucked from the club. I'm totally dreading it.

After lunch, I'm at my locker when an announcement comes over the PA system.

"All students are to report immediately to their homerooms for attendance. Then proceed directly to the gym."

Another assembly? I look around. Like everyone else, I have no idea what this is about. And just like last time,

I go to the gym by myself. I keep wishing I was there with Amira and the rest of my former friends.

We're hardly settled in the gym when Ms. Chen starts to speak. "Welcome, students and staff," she says. "I recently spoke to you about some troubling events within our community and at our school. Today, I want to share some further news with everyone.

"First of all," Ms. Chen continues, "as many of you know, Mrs. Rashid suffered a fall outside Fairview Court several days ago. Mrs. Rashid has been a good friend to Addison, and I've been in touch with her daughter. She reports that Mrs. Rashid is recovering well from her surgery. Her doctor believes she will make a full recovery."

My eyes well up with tears at those words. My first instinct is to look over at Amira. I miss her and the others from the club more than ever.

Amira catches my eye. She smiles and gives me a thumbs-up. I smile back. Maybe this is a start.

"There has been some speculation as to what actually happened," Ms. Chen continues. "And, as you know, I'm not fond of speculation."

Some students squirm in their seats.

"Since Mrs. Rashid was unable to tell us herself, we didn't know the facts. Or, at least, we didn't know until now."

I sit up straighter in my chair, my stomach filled with butterflies.

"Fairview Court and the outdoor area surrounding it is monitored electronically. Video surveillance is helpful for matters of general security. It's also helpful for maintaining resident safety—for example, if Fairview residents who suffer from memory problems begin to wander." Ms. Chen pushes her glasses up. "To rule out any foul play, the police reviewed the footage. They have now authorized me to share their findings."

I take a deep breath and hold it in. *Please don't say Jude did it.* I repeat the words over and over.

"The video shows that Mrs. Rashid was alone at the time of her fall. It was 100 percent accidental. I do not wish to minimize in any way how serious her injury was. I'm relieved, however, that nobody was to blame for it."

Oh, thank goodness! Thank goodness it wasn't the group-home kids—or anyone else—who hurt her. And thank goodness it wasn't Jude.

A moment later the guilt kicks in. Jude told me he didn't do it. Still, I doubted him right up to this moment.

"Fortunately, she wasn't alone for long," Ms. Chen continues. "The video clearly shows an employee finding Mrs. Rashid very soon after her fall."

Exactly like Jude said.

"And thankfully, as I mentioned," Ms. Chen says, "Mrs. Rashid is recovering well."

At that point, applause breaks out in some parts of the gym. Ms. Chen waits for the students to quiet down before she continues.

"I also need to inform you that the group home, known by many of us as the Blue House, has been shut down."

My breath catches.

"I can't tell you how sad this makes me," Ms. Chen says. "The teens from the group home behaved as responsible members of our community. Yet right from the outset, some adults in our community, along with students here at Addison, jumped to conclusions about them. Many people made those teenagers feel terribly unwelcome."

As her words sink in, a heavy silence falls over the gym.

"Those teenagers deserved to be treated better," Ms. Chen continues. "I particularly expect that of you people—our younger generation. Otherwise, the future I think we *all* wish for is at risk." She pauses and looks hard around the gym. "As it stands, the students from the Blue House will no longer be attending our school."

I feel like I have been dropped in cold water. So Jude has left? Even though he told me he was probably going to change schools, I kept hoping he wouldn't.

"At this time, it is unclear whether the Blue House will reopen. I remain hopeful, however, that that will be the case. And now I have a few final announcements to make."

Oh no! What can she possibly have left to tell us?

"After a locker search," Ms. Chen continues, "the person responsible for the graffiti has been caught. This student also confessed to some other acts of vandalism, including the destruction of the park bench the Unity Club worked so hard to raise funds for. I believe it is important to stress that the individual who caused those damages was *not* one of the teenagers living at the group home."

Some murmurs run through the crowd at this news.

"Plus," Ms. Chen says, "it has not gone unnoticed that even some members of the Unity Club—the very group committed to fostering social responsibility, compassion and inclusion—were quick to blame the teens from the Blue House."

I glance over at Amira and the rest of the Unity Club members. Some have slid down in their chairs, their heads down. It looks like they are trying to makes themselves as small as possible.

"I would like each and every one of you to go home tonight and try to imagine what life is like for the teenagers who were living there. I want you to think about the challenges they face, and about how easily their circumstances could be yours." Ms. Chen pauses. "And then let's all start fresh tomorrow being kind to one another, especially to those less fortunate than we are."

It takes me a moment to realize that everyone is standing up and leaving the gym. I'm wiping my eyes when someone gives my hand a squeeze. A warm, comforting squeeze, followed by a hug.

"She's going to be okay," Amira says. "Mrs. Rashid will be okay."

"Yes." I hug her back. I'm too choked up to say anything else.

Amira steps back, and we give each other teary smiles. "And Jude and the others didn't do it." A sheepish look crosses her face. "I'm sorry, Brett. I just really thought that—"

"I know," I say. "I was starting to think that too."

"Really?" Amira asks.

I take a deep breath. "I'm glad we were both wrong."

Chapter Fifteen

At the next meeting, Tassie updates us on the work being done with the environmental program. "Suresh, Georgia and I spoke with Ms. Chen. She approved our plans for the Earth Day celebration. And the PA announcements for this week will focus on how students can make more earth-friendly food choices."

"We've posted ideas on the website too," Georgia adds.

"Well done, you guys," I say. "And how about Mini Gym Kids?" I try not to think about how much fun we had when Jude joined us. "It looks like their numbers are still growing. Who can help out this week?"

I am relieved that enough people volunteer so I can skip it this week. If Mrs. Rashid is up for visitors, I'd really like to go visit her at the hospital instead.

"Now that we've covered our usual business," I say, "there's one new item I'd like to talk about. But first I want to thank Kaden for running the last meeting for me."

Kaden looks up and gives what is almost a smile.

"When Isabelle moved away and we needed a new club president, I was so thrilled that the group trusted me in this position," I say. "But I was so thrilled that I overlooked something important. The best thing about this club is the different perspectives we all bring to it. For that reason, I've made a decision. Some of you"—I look at Kaden—"felt strongly that there could only be one president. But I feel just as strongly that this club needs more than one leader. Also," I continue, "sometimes I need a break. Like, to address some stuff with my family."

Not even Amira knows that ever since my mom moved away, I've been keeping extra busy to avoid thinking about her. But now it seems like some extra thinking time—maybe to knit some of my own projects, or write down my thoughts in a journal—might be a healthier way to cope.

"I'd very much like to stay on as one of those presidents. And as your current president, I would like to nominate Kaden to be co-president. He has lots of experience with the Unity Club. He also has a different perspective that would complement mine. So if anyone has a problem with us working together…"

Nobody says anything for a moment. But then some cheers go up around the room. Some people are clapping Kaden on the back. The relief I'm feeling, along with the smile on Kaden's face, tells me I made the right call.

As for that big blue house, I'll figure out what I think about that—and maybe even about my mom—in the days ahead.

Every time I've walked by the house this week, I've looked directly at it. No more turning away. I've also bought a new journal. I'm using it to write down my thoughts about the house. For the whole time my mom lived there, it felt like a home to me. I hope it felt like home to Jude and to the other kids who lived there too. But how do I feel about the house now that it no longer connects me to Maman? I'm still trying to figure that out.

It's Saturday morning, and because I have some extra time, I've read all of my mom's texts. Now I know she is enjoying her new job in Winnipeg. She's still dating Zoltan, but they've decided they need some space. She has her own apartment now, and it has a second bedroom. She wants me to go visit her there over the next long weekend. I'm not sure how I feel about that yet.

My phone buzzes. Surprisingly, it's not my mom. It's Jude.

Hey! Wanna meet downtown this aft? Hot chocolate?

That sounds like fun. I text him back right away.

Sure. Where?

Jude mentions a coffee shop downtown. I could take the bus there. But because Papa hasn't been working quite so much lately, he offers to drive me. I think maybe he wants to meet Jude for himself. Papa even calls it a "date," which it totally isn't. I correct him about that right away.

I finally agree to let him drive me, but I ask him to drop me off a block away from the coffee shop. I don't want to freak Jude out.

"I can pick you up later," Papa says.

"*Non*," I say. "That's okay. I don't know how long I'll be here. I'll take the bus home later."

Papa frowns in a way that tells me this isn't his ideal choice. "Okay," he says. "*À bientôt*."

"See you soon, Papa."

Chapter Sixteen

Jude isn't at the coffee shop when I get there. So I grab a booth and pull out my journal and pen. I'm rereading a poem I've been working on when Jude arrives. I smile when I see he's wearing the cable scarf.

"Oh, hey." I tuck everything back into my bag. We both go to the counter to order our hot chocolates.

"Were you doing homework?" Jude asks as we slide back into the booth.

"No," I say. "Just some of my own writing."

"Cool," Jude says. "How's everything going at Addison?"

"Things are good." I take a sip of my drink. "Ms. Chen called an assembly. Everyone knows now that you guys from the Blue House didn't have anything to do with Mrs. Rashid getting hurt. Or with the vandalism around the neighborhood."

I pause before I say this next part. "So the coast is clear for you to come back. If you want to, that is."

Jude pauses for a moment, then shakes his head. "I can't go back," he says. "That feeling of people watching you all the time, like they're just waiting for you to do something wrong or illegal…I didn't like it. Not at all."

"That makes sense," I say. "Still, you didn't do anything."

"Thanks for saying that." Jude takes another drink of his hot chocolate. "You know, I'm getting pretty settled in with my new foster family. This one seems really nice."

I nod. "Will you be living with them for long?"

"I think so," Jude says. "Assuming it works out okay."

"So you don't have any other family?" Then I realize I've asked too much. "Sorry," I say. "That's none of my business."

"It's okay," Jude says. "You've already met my older brother, Ricardo. Or you sort of met him. Ricardo was at Beans Bistro with me a few times when you were there too." Jude blushes. "He gets pretty heated sometimes."

I flash back to Jude trying to shush the guy waving his hands around.

"Yeah," I say. "I remember him."

Jude nods. "The last few years have been hard for us," he says. "Our mom died of cancer three years ago. After all we survived while we were living in Haiti, I can't believe that's what happened to her after we finally moved away.

"Before my mom died, she made Ricardo and me promise to look after each other. She knew our dad wouldn't be able to do it. He has bipolar disorder. He's been hospitalized off and on for years."

Jude seems to get lost in his own thoughts. I want to say something to help, but I don't know what to say at all. So I just wait.

"Ricardo has mostly been living on friends' couches and on the street since our mom died. He sometimes came around the group home to check in on me. He doesn't always make good choices."

I remember Jude bolting out the door when he got that text at Beans. I wonder what kind of trouble he was trying to keep Ricardo out of that night.

"So I guess you won't be coming back to Addison." My voice shakes a bit. It's great that I'm friends again with Amira and the rest of the Unity Club. But I'll miss Jude.

"No," Jude says. "But actually, my new school and foster home are pretty close to where we went with the Unity Club. You know, to play dodgeball with those little kids? That was a fun time, right?"

He doesn't wait for an answer. "While I was playing with them, I remembered what it was like to be that little and that happy again."

"Yeah, I get that," I say. "And you know, we still need more people to help out there. It doesn't matter that you aren't a student at Addison."

"Are you sure?"

"Yeah," I say. "It'd be great if you could join us there again."

The whole time we've been talking, my eyes keep drifting to the cable scarf. Jude smiles and holds up an end of it.

"I figured out a while ago that you made this," he says. "I like it a lot. But if it's okay with you, I'd really like to give it to someone."

"Really?"

"Yeah," Jude says. "I've been thinking about this for a while. I'd like to give it to Ricardo. He's living rough most of the time. He really needs it more than I do. But I wanted to check with you first."

I think about the cable pattern. About how it symbolizes a rope or a lifeline that brings people back home to safety. Maybe it can do that for Ricardo.

"I don't mind at all," I say. "Actually, I'd really like that." I look down at my empty cup. "So will you come to Mini Gym Kids on Tuesday after school?"

"I think that'll be okay," Jude says. "I'll text you later and let you know for sure."

We leave the coffee shop. Jude waits with me at the bus stop. It seems we're both talked out, because we just stand there and don't say anything. Somehow, though, that feels okay.

When the bus comes, we say goodbye. And when it pulls out, I wave to Jude. He smiles and waves back. Then he holds up his phone and points to it.

What? I mouth the word to him through the bus window.

Before the bus turns the corner, I see him texting. Moments later his message arrives.

Text your mom, okay?

I think about how Jude can't text his mom. He no longer has that option.

But I do. As the bus moves down the street, I decide to take his advice.

Bonjour, Maman. **We have a lot to talk about.**

Acknowledgments

Without the support of others, I could not have brought this book to life. My thanks, first of all, to Allen Balser, who answered my many questions about group homes for youths. Allen's kindness and generosity are great gifts to me. I also wish to thank Shannon Fitz, whose passion for community service and volunteerism with the Interact Club at *École Ross Sheppard* helped inspire this story. Anna Fitz continues to double-check my written French for me—just in case. *Merci beaucoup pour ton aide, Anna*. Gratitude also to Paul Spafford, accomplished cook and brother, whose earliest method of varying his diet crept into my story. My thanks, of course, to the Orca pod for their confidence in me. I am especially indebted to Tanya Trafford, whose editorial feedback strengthened this book immeasurably.

And as always, I am incredibly grateful to have the most supportive family in the world. *Je vous aime, Ken, Anna et Shannon.*

Karen Spafford-Fitz worked as a swimming instructor and lifeguard, an aquatics director and a junior-high teacher before discovering her passion for writing. She is now the author of several novels for young people, including *Vanish* and *Dog Walker* in the Orca Currents series. When she is not writing in her studio in Edmonton, Alberta, Karen is often training for her next half marathon with her beloved German shepherd. For more information, visit karenspafford-fitz.com.

For more information on all the books
in the Orca Currents series, please visit
orcabook.com.